© 1995 Twin Books Ltd

Produced by
TWIN BOOKS
Kimbolton House
117a Fulham Road
London SW3 6RL

Directed by CND – Muriel Nathan-Deiller
Illustrated by Van Gool-Lefèvre-Loiseaux

ISBN: 1 85469 778 1

Printed in China

Peter Pan

Van Gool

TWIN BOOKS

It was a dark night in London, and Mr and Mrs Darling, helped by Nana the dog, were putting their children to bed. "Come on, children it's time to go to bed," said Mrs Darling. "Look, Mummy, Peter Pan has been flying in here!" exclaimed Wendy, the eldest. "Here are some leaves from his suit. Peter, where are you?" "In Never-Never Land!" shouted John and Michael.

"That's enough, now settle down and no more nonsense about flying boys. You must go to sleep," said Mr Darling, as he left the nursery.

Later that evening Mrs Darling was sitting in the children's room sewing. It was so quiet that she had fallen asleep, but suddenly she was awoken by the rustle of leaves. She opened her eyes and let out a cry: there was a boy flying around the room!

Nana chased the flying boy out of the window.
Before he could escape, Nana caught hold of
Peter Pan's shadow.

Later that night, Peter Pan returned through the open window to find his lost shadow. This time he had brought his friend, Tinkerbell, the fairy. She was so small that all you could see of her when she flew was a bright sparkling light.

Peter found his shadow hiding in the nursery. But as hard as he tried he couldn't stick it back to his feet. The bubbles from the soap he was using as glue soon filled the air.

Just then Wendy woke up, because of all the noise Peter was making.

"Oh, Peter you're back! Come here with your shadow, and I'll sew it back on for you." When she was finished Peter gave Wendy a necklace as a thank you present. "Peter, it's lovely!" exclaimed Wendy. Suddenly she saw the flickering light that had arrived with Peter. "Wendy, this is Tinkerbell," said Peter.

Peter Pan was so pleased to have his shadow back that he asked Wendy to come with him to Never Never Land.

Wendy woke John and Michael. "We're going to Never Never Land with Peter! Come on!" Tinkerbell sprinkled them all with glittering pixie dust and the children rose into the air. They flew out of the nursery window, and over the rooftops of London.

After a long time in the air the small group arrived at Never Never Land. "Go on Tinker, you lead the way. It's so dark. . . ." said Peter. Suddenly – WHIZZZ! A red light flashed across the sky. "A cannon ball! Watch out Wendy, the pirates are firing at us." But the warning came too late and they were separated.

Wendy was lost in the sky above Never Never Land with Tinkerbell. "I will leave her," thought Tinkerbell. "She wants to take Peter away from me!" With that she flew straight to the Lost Boys. "What's that Tinkerbell? Peter wants us to shoot down a great white bird?" Keen to obey Peter's wishes, the Lost Boys picked up their bows and arrows.

Wendy was hit by one of the arrows and fell to the ground. "What have you done?" asked Peter when he arrived back. "I was bringing you a mother to tell you stories and you've killed her!"

"But Peter, Tinkerbell said that you wanted us to knock her out of the sky," protested one of the Lost Boys. "Tinkerbell, how could you? Go away! I never want to see you again!"

23

Just then Wendy began to move her arm, and gradually she sat up. "She's alive!" whispered the Lost Boys. "Peter's necklace must have protected me," said Wendy. There was a shuffling behind her. John and Michael had arrived too. Two new friends and a mother! The Lost Boys were very happy and took everyone back to their hideaway.

From then on, Wendy took charge of the Lost Boys. During the day, Peter showed Wendy and her brothers the island sights. He took them to meet the mermaids who took a strong dislike to Wendy as soon as they saw her.

"Send her away, Peter, then we can play," they called out rudely.

Wendy was a little upset at being disliked so much before she had even had a chance to speak!

Suddenly Peter hissed, "Look!" and whispered to Wendy and the others, "Pirates! They've captured the Indian Chief's daughter, Tiger Lily. Quick, we must help!"

"They are going to tie her to that rock – she'll drown at high tide!" exclaimed Wendy. Hiding behind a rock, Peter imitated Captain Hook's voice. "Release Tiger Lily!"

"But Captain, you said. . . . . . ."

"I've changed my plans. Just do as you're told!" The two pirates let Tiger Lily go, and she jumped into the water and swam for the shore.

The real Captain Hook arrived at that moment. "Where is Tiger Lily?" he demanded.

"Hello, Hook!" said Peter Pan, appearing before him. "I've let Tiger Lily go!"

Hook was furious that yet another of his wicked plans had gone wrong because of Peter Pan. He drew his sword and a terrible fight began.

Chasing over the rocks after Hook, Peter slipped and fell. Captain Hook bashed him on the head with his hook, and ran away to his ship. He hoped that Peter would be drowned when the tide came in. "Revenge at last," he thought.

But Wendy, who had been watching everything from behind a rock, came to Peter's rescue. "How are we going to get home?" she wondered out loud. "You're too weak to fly and I'm not strong enough to support you."

They stayed there for some time while Peter slept. The water was slowly rising up the rock. Suddenly Wendy saw something floating towards them. It was a kite! "This will help me carry Peter!" she thought in delight. Reaching out, she caught hold of the string. Peter just managed to hold on to Wendy as the kite lifted them away from the rocks.

Wendy and Peter arrived back safely. While Peter rested, Wendy told the Lost Boys another story. She was missing her parents and so she told the Lost Boys all about them.

"Why don't you come back to London with us?" she suggested. "I'm sure our parents will look after you." The Lost Boys were very excited. "I want to stay here," said Peter sadly, "I don't want to grow up."

The Lost Boys, Wendy, John and Michael
filed out of the hideaway ready to fly to the
Darling home. But the pirates were waiting for
them. "Tie them up!" shouted Captain Hook.
"Peter! Help us!" cried Michael.
"What's this? Peter Pan is alive?" spluttered
the angry Captain, "Take the prisoners to the
ship. This time I'm really going to finish him
off."

Hook tied Wendy to the mast and held John and Michael prisoner. Suddenly Peter flew on to the ship. He cut the ropes that were tied around Michael and John and then released Wendy. Captain Hook nearly fainted with shock. A crocodile was waiting nearby, eyeing the ship hopefully.

Hook cowered in the background while the children fought the pirates. Wendy and her brothers chased them around the ship until they were exhausted. Peter flew at Hook who lost his balance and tumbled into the sea, where the crocodile was waiting for him.

After their victory, Wendy announced that she still wanted to go home. Peter agreed to show them the way. "The Lost Boys can stay with you if they want, but I'm going to come back here to Never Never Land," declared Peter.

What a surprise for Mr & Mrs Darling when they saw their children's new friends!

43

The Darlings agreed to let
the Lost Boys stay.
"And Peter?" whispered
Wendy, watching him fly
away. "I'll come back for
you once a year, Wendy,"
cried Peter. "For a holiday
in Never Never Land!"